DC SUPER FRIENDS

BRAIN FREEZE!

BRAIN FREEZE!
A BANTAM BOOK 978 0 857 51185 0

Published in Great Britain by Bantam, an imprint of Random House Children's Publishers UK
A Random House Group Company

This edition published 2013

1 3 5 7 9 10 8 6 4 2

Copyright © 2013 DC Comics.
DC SUPER FRIENDS and all related characters
and elements are trademarks of and © DC Comics.
WB SHIELD: ™ & © Warner Bros. Entertainment Inc.
(s12)

RHUK 28471

Bantam Books are published by Random House Children's Publishers UK,
61–63 Uxbridge Road, London W5 5SA

www.**randomhousechildrens**.co.uk

Addresses for companies within The Random House Group Limited can be found at:
www.randomhouse.co.uk/offices.htm

THE RANDOM HOUSE GROUP Limited Reg. No. 954009

A CIP catalogue record for this book is available from the British Library

Printed in China

The Random House Group Limited supports The Forest Stewardship Council® (FSC®), the leading
international forest certification organization. Our books carrying the FSC label are printed on
FSC®-certified paper. FSC is the only forest certification scheme endorsed by the leading
environmental organizations, including Greenpeace. Our paper procurement policy can be
found at www.randomhouse.co.uk/environment

DC SUPER FRIENDS™

BRAIN FREEZE!

By J. E. Bright

Illustrated by Loston Wallace and David Tanguay

BANTAM BOOKS

It is a big day
in Metropolis.

A new computer will control everything.

The computer is
called the Brain.
It will run the trains.

It will control
the traffic lights,
the water supply
and the power.

Superman pulls the
switch that turns
on the Brain.

Mr. Freeze wants
to give Metropolis
brain freeze!

Mr. Freeze fires

his ice cannon.

The Brain is
frozen solid!

The city's water stops running.

The power
goes off.

A train speeds
out of control!

Superman and the Flash
zoom into action.

Superman stops

the train.

The Flash helps
the passengers.

Cyborg tells the cars when to stop.

Green Lantern tells
them when to go.

Batman swings down
towards Mr. Freeze.

Mr. Freeze uses his ice blaster!

Batman's feet
become frozen.

Superman breaks the ice.

Batman smashes

the ice blaster.

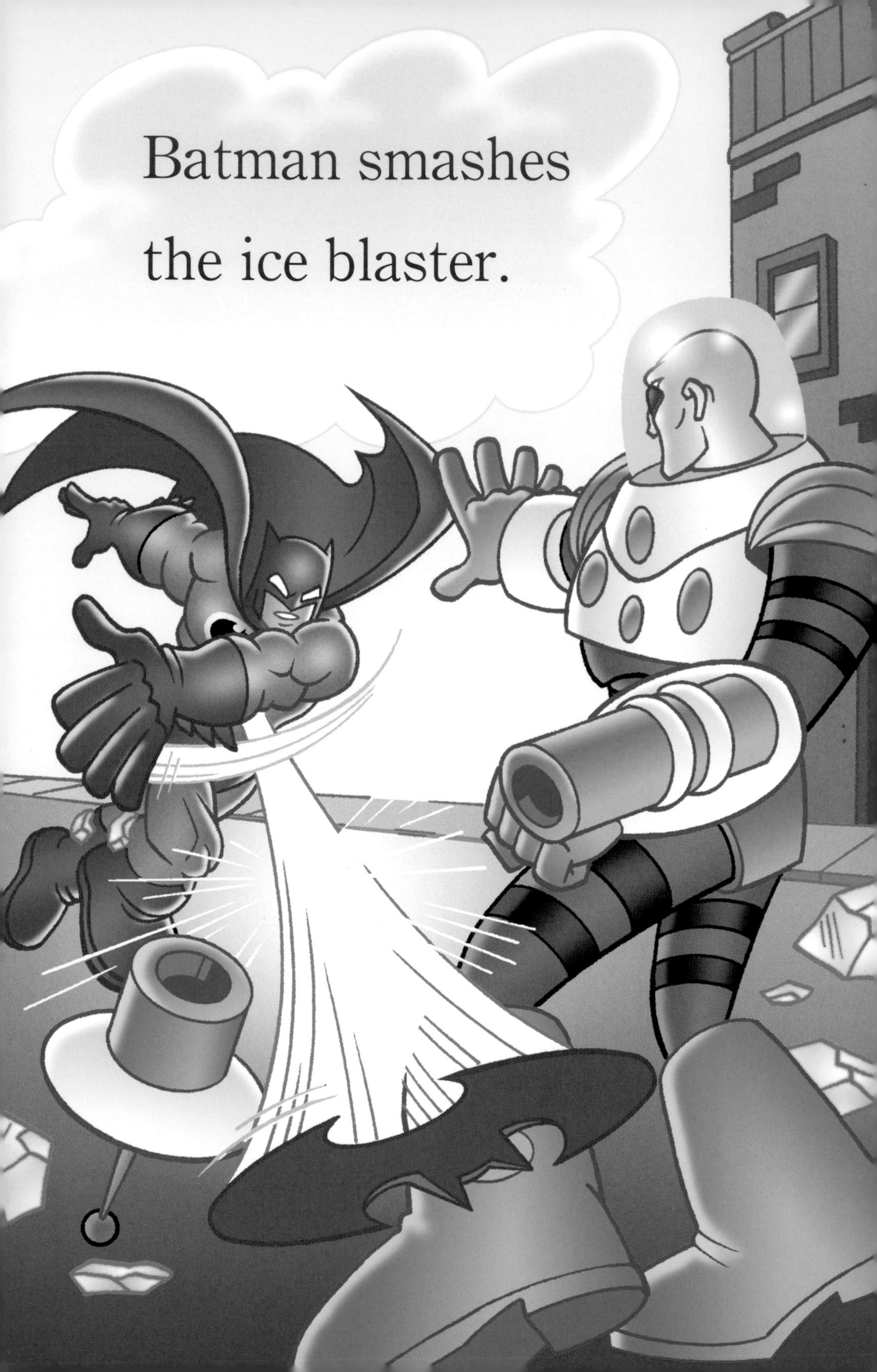

Mr. Freeze runs
to his ice cannon!

Superman uses
his heat vision
to melt the cannon.

Superman thaws

the Brain.

It still works!

Teamwork saves
the city.

The Super Friends celebrate with ice cream!